A Lei for Tutu

by Rebecca Nevers Fellows

illustrated by Linda Finch

Albert Whitman & Company, Morton Grove, Illinois

For my 'ohana, always. And for Jessica, Aloha nui loa. —R.N.F.

For Mitch, with much love and gratitude. —L.F.

Thanks to the following people for so generously sharing their time and expertise: Naomi Carter, Culture and Arts Section, Honolulu Parks and Recreation Department, Honolulu, Hawai'i; Nancy Holt, Cultural Resources Specialist, Bernice P. Bishop Museum, Honolulu, Hawai'i; Don and Ruthie Schultz; and Frank O. Hay.

Library of Congress Cataloging-in-Publication Data

Fellows, Rebecca Nevers.
A lei for Tutu / by Rebecca Nevers Fellows; illustrated by Linda Finch.
p. cm.
Summary: Nāhoa loves making lei with her grandmother and looks forward to helping
her create a special one for Lei Day, until her grandmother becomes very ill.
ISBN 0-8075-4426-4
[1. Leis—Fiction. 2. Grandmothers—Fiction. 3. Hawaii—Fiction.] I. Finch, Linda, ill. II. Title.
PZ7.F3364Lf 1998 [E]—dc21 98-9319
CIP AC

Text copyright © 1998 by Rebecca Nevers Fellows.
Illustrations copyright © 1998 by Linda Finch.
Published in 1998 by Albert Whitman & Company, 6340 Oakton Street, Morton Grove, Illinois 60053-2723.
Published simultaneously in Canada by General Publishing, Limited, Toronto.
Printed in the United States of America.
10 9 8 7 6 5 4 3 2 1

The illustrations were rendered in watercolors.
The design is by Scott Piehl.

Albert Whitman & Company is also the publisher of The Boxcar Children® Mysteries.
For more information about all our fine books, visit us at www.awhitmanco.com.

About Lei Day

The custom of Lei Day began in the 1920s, before Hawai'i was even a state. Don Blanding, an American poet and newspaperman who had settled in Hawai'i, is credited with being the creator of Lei Day. Having the true "spirit of aloha"—a warm and loving feeling—for his new home, Mr. Blanding wanted to establish a day when lei would be freely worn and exchanged. He and some enthusiastic friends decided to celebrate the first Lei Day on the first of May in 1927. The event became popular, and within a few years Lei Day was officially recognized by Honolulu City Hall with a pageant and lei exhibition.

Today, the Honolulu Parks and Recreation Department sponsors the much-loved Lei Day Festival. The pageant highlights the lei of the eight islands of Hawai'i. A lei queen is chosen, and each of the eight islands is represented by a princess wearing a lei and a haloku (long dress) of that island's color. Many elements of Hawai'i's culture are celebrated, including music, hula, kapa-cloth making, and other ancient arts. "Pageant fever" can be found all over the community and especially in schools, as children take part in their own festivities honoring Hawai'ian costumes, arts, and crafts.

The lei competition is one of the most popular events. People of all ages and from many walks of life, from all the Hawai'ian islands, enter the contest. The hours of work involved, the beauty and variety of flowers used, and the skill of the lei makers ensure that the competing lei are true works of art.

Nāhoa's eyes flew open. She lay still for a moment, feeling the trade winds blow soft and warm through her window. She smiled as she watched a gecko scamper across her wall.

"I get to work with Tutu at her lei stand today!" she said, remembering. "We will finish planning her lei for the Lei Day contest. It will be her most nani lei yet!"

plumeria

As she got dressed, Nāhoa thought of last year's Lei Day festival. Mrs. Silva and Mrs. Keha, who owned the lei stands right next to Tutu's, had entered their best lei. Tutu had made a beautiful lei, all shades of red.

But the judges had pinned the Mayor's Grand Prize ribbon next to Mrs. Keha's lei!

Tutu and Nāhoa had been so disappointed.

Nāhoa knew this year would be different. She pictured the flowers they would use, and the shiny green and gently fragrant maile. She could clearly see the pua kalaunu, a favorite of Queen Lili'oukalani. She could even see the waioleka, the small blue violets loved by the paniolo, those Hawai'ian cowboys.

Nāhoa raced to the kitchen for her breakfast of poi and banana. She knew Tutu Pualani would be sipping her coffee, a bright red hibiscus blossom tucked behind her ear. She would be wearing her favorite muʻumuʻu, all swirls of blue and green, and her bright smile.

Instead, Nāhoa found only her mother and her Uncle Keawe at the table, speaking in low voices. Her mother was crying.

"It's Tutu, Nāhoa," Uncle Keawe said. "Her heart's gone sick, and she's in the hospital."

Her heart? How could Tutu Pualani's big, warm heart get sick?

"I want to see her, Mama!" Nāhoa cried. "Please!"

Uncle Keawe looked at Mama. "I'll get the truck," he said.

hibiscus

Nāhoa sat between Uncle Keawe and Mama on the ride to the hospital. Mama patted her hand.

"Tutu will be all right," she said.

At the hospital, Nāhoa stepped through the door Mama opened for her. Tutu lay very still, eyes closed, long gray hair fanned out onto her pillow. Tubes connected her to a humming machine.

"Tutu?" Nāhoa whispered.

waioleka

pua kalaunu

The old woman's eyes opened, and she turned her head toward them.

"Aloha, my punahele! You've come to visit me!"

Nāhoa ran to hug her grandmother.

"How is my lei stand?" Tutu asked.

"I'm going to help cousin Malina there, every afternoon!"

Tutu smiled. "I'm sorry we won't be making our Lei Day lei."

"It would have been beautiful, Tutu," said Nāhoa.

For a moment Tutu's eyes brightened. Her voice sounded strong. "The way we planned to use the waioleka and pua kalaunu would have been so striking! It would have been my best lei yet—I'm sure of it!"

"Enough talk about lei," Mama said to Tutu. "You need to rest."

For the next week, Mama spent every day with Tutu. After school Nāhoa would race home and ask, "How is she today?" And Mama would answer, "Still not so good, Nāhoa."

But that changed each evening at visiting hours when Nāhoa burst through Tutu's door.

"What lei did you make today?" Tutu would ask excitedly. "Is Malina buying only the best flowers? Are the plumeria blossoms very fresh?"

Then visiting hours would end, and as Nāhoa watched sadly, Tutu would sink back quietly onto her pillow.

One evening, on the drive home, Nāhoa had an idea.

"Tutu should be making lei."

"What?" Mama asked, surprised.

"Tutu needs to make lei," Nāhoa repeated. "It would make her happy again."

"You can't be serious, Nāhoa," Mama said sternly. "Tutu needs lots of rest, not to be making lei!"

"I just think—"

"Nāhoa!" said Mama. "You think you know more than Dr. Ramos what Tutu needs?"

Nāhoa folded her arms across her chest.

"Yes," she said, so softly no one heard her.

The next day at the lei stand, Malina put Nāhoa to work.

"The vanda orchids are in the red box in the refrigerator, Nāhoa," she said. "Use them to string more lei."

Near the vandas were boxes filled with maile, pua kalaunu, and waioleka.

Why, these were all Tutu's Lei Day flowers!

Nāhoa had another idea.

vanda orchid

For the rest of the day, as Nāhoa strung lei, she kept a basket near her feet. Anytime she came upon an especially pretty blossom or piece of greenery, she would sneak it into the basket.

"What are you doing there, Nāhoa?" Malina asked her once, eyes narrowed.

"Oh, nothing, Malina," said Nāhoa. "Just finishing up one last lei!"

At the end of the day, Nāhoa's basket was filled with the beautiful flowers and greens that Tutu liked best. While Malina locked up, Nāhoa hurried her treasure to the truck.

"What's all this?" asked Uncle Keawe.

"It's for Tutu," Nāhoa said. "But I need your help!"

In a little while, they were on their way to the hospital.

"Ah, Nāhoa, I shouldn't be doing this! Your mother will be so angry with me!" Uncle Keawe said.

But Nāhoa's mind was made up. Tomorrow was Lei Day; she had to get the flowers to Tutu.

maile

In the hospital room, Nāhoa called softly, "Tutu? It's Nāhoa."
Tutu Pualani opened her eyes.
"Tutu, look what we've brought you!" Nāhoa held out the basket.
She pulled back the damp newspaper she had used to keep the
flowers fresh. The blossoms glistened, their fragrance filling the
room.
  Tutu sat straight up. Her eyes sparkled.
  "Nāhoa! You have brought the flowers for our lei!"

They immediately set to work—Tutu sewing and Nāhoa handing her the blossoms. So intent were they on the lei, they didn't hear the door open.

Dr. Ramos looked surprised. He placed his stethoscope on Tutu's chest, moving it from here to there. All at once, a grin broke across his face.

"That's a beautiful lei, Pualani," he said, and winked at Nāhoa. "I'm glad to see you so happy again."

Nāhoa smiled, for Tutu's face glowed as it used to.

"Why, we may even have to let you go home!"

"Once the lei is all pau," said Uncle Keawe, "I have an important delivery to make!"

On Lei Day, Uncle Keawe drove Mama, Tutu, and Nāhoa to Kapiʻolani Park. The big Hawaiʻian sun shone brightly on all the festivities. Women pounded bark for kapa cloth while girls in ti leaf skirts danced the hula. Ancient Hawaiʻian chants and music filled the air. All the beautiful lei were hung, waiting to be judged.

Nāhoa saw Mrs. Silva's lei and Mrs. Keha's lei.

"There's Tutu's lei!" said Uncle Keawe, pointing.

"Why, what's this?" exclaimed Mama, turning to Nāhoa.

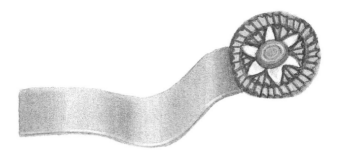

"It's a surprise, Mama!"

"Yes, dear," said Tutu. "Please don't be angry with Nāhoa."

"Hush!" said Uncle Keawe. "The judges are coming!"

Nāhoa held her breath. The judges walked by Mrs. Silva's lei. They stopped. They walked to Mrs. Keha's lei. They wrote in their notebooks.

They gathered before Tutu's lei and whispered to each other.

Then they pinned the Mayor's Grand Prize right next to Tutu Pualani's lei!

"Tutu!" exclaimed Nāhoa. "You did it!"

Tutu Pualani turned to Nāhoa, her smile brighter than the sun.

"No, my punahele," she said. "We did it. Together."

Making Your Own Lei

While it is a lot of fun to make a fresh flower lei, gathering enough blossoms can be a problem. Here is an easy "lei pepa," or paper lei, you can give to your friends on Lei Day.

What you need:

1. One seven-yard strip of crepe paper.
    (It comes in rolls of twenty-four yards.)

2. A yardstick or measuring tape

3. A large sewing needle

4. A spool of thread. It can be the color of the crepe paper or any
    color you like.

What to do:

1. Cut a seven-yard strip of crepe paper.

2. Thread your needle with about a yard of thread. You may want to
    double the thread to make it stronger. Make a big knot at the end.

3. Make a big running stitch down the middle of the crepe paper.

4. After stitching for two or three inches, twist the crepe paper and
    push it along the thread toward the knot, gathering it. Stitch
    another two or three inches, twist the paper in the opposite
    direction, and gather it some more.

5. Continue to stitch, twist, and gather until you have used all the paper.

6. Remove the needle and tie the thread ends together.

7. Add a ribbon bow, if you like.

8. Wear your lei with the spirit of aloha!

Glossary

aloha   (uh-LOH-uh) love; warm, friendly greeting or farewell

gecko   (GEHK-oh) a small nocturnal lizard

hibiscus   (hy-BIHS-kuhs) The state flower of Hawai'i. The hibiscus is usually red, pink, peach, yellow, or white.

hula   (HOO-lah) an ancient form of expression that tells a story through dance

kapa (or tapa)   (KAH-pah) an unwoven cloth made from the inner bark of the paper mulberry tree

lei   (lay) a garland of flowers, shells, leaves, feathers, papers, or other materials worn around the neck or head. The plural form of the word is also lei.

maile   (MY-lay) a shiny, fragrant, green leafy vine

mu'umu'u   (moo oo-MOO oo) a loose gown

Nāhoa   (NA-hoh-uh) a Hawai'ian name meaning "bold" or "defiant"

nani   (NAH-nee) beautiful

paniolo   (pah-nee-OH-lo) a Hawai'ian cowboy

pau   (pow) finished; done

plumeria   (ploo-MEER-ee-uh) a common, very fragrant blossom first introduced to Hawai'i from the Orient in the late 1800s. Plumeria may be white, yellow, pink, red, or striped.

poi   (poy) a staple of Hawai'ian diet, made from a plant called taro (TAH-roh). Its underground stems are cooked, pounded until smooth, and thinned with water.

pua kalaunu   (poo-ah kah-LAH-noo) the crownflower. It has small lavender or white flowers.

punahele   (poo-nah-HAY-lay) favorite one; "my pet"

Queen Lili'uokalani   (lil-li oo-o-kah-lah-nee) Hawai'i's last monarch, who reigned from January 29, 1891, until she was overthrown on January 17, 1893

ti   (tee) woody plant with large, broad green leaves

Tutu   (TOO-too) nickname for Grandmother

vanda   (VAN-dah) a type of orchid

waioleka   (why-o-LAY-kah) a kind of violet